The Magic Secrets Box

The Great Mermaid Rescue

To Kayleigh Adams
with lots of love
~ *SM*

With special thanks to ML
~ *AD*

STRIPES PUBLISHING
An imprint of Magi Publications
1 The Coda Centre, 189 Munster Road,
London SW6 6AW

A paperback original
First published in Great Britain in 2011

Text copyright © Sue Mongredien, 2011
Illustrations copyright © Artful Doodlers, 2011
Music supplied under licence & copyright © N J Dean & Co, 2011

ISBN: 978-1-84715-185-8

A CIP catalogue record for this book is available
from the British Library.

Printed and bound in China.

STP/1800/0006/0511

2 4 6 8 10 9 7 5 3 1

The
Great Mermaid Rescue

SUE MONGREDIEN

The Magic Secrets Box

Chapter One

"Megan Andrews, have you listened to a single word I've said?" came the cross voice of Mrs Harvey, her teacher.

Megan jerked out of her daydream guiltily. She'd completely forgotten she was at school. "Um … yes," she said after a moment, although that wasn't strictly true. The fact was, daydreaming about her recent adventure in the Land of Eight Kingdoms was way more interesting than learning about the Victorians.

Mrs Harvey's eyes narrowed. "Hmm," she said. "Well, try to look as if you're listening, at least. Don't just sit there gazing out of the window. Now, in Victorian times…"

Megan tried to concentrate as her teacher began droning on again, but it was almost impossible to stop her mind drifting. Incredible as it may sound, the Fairy Queen from the Land of Eight Kingdoms was at that very moment in Megan's bedroom, trapped inside her music box. How was anyone meant to think about boring old Victorians when they'd recently made friends with a real Fairy Queen?

Last Saturday had been the most exciting day of Megan's life, from the moment she'd spotted the old music

box in a second-hand shop and felt
compelled to buy it. Back home, when
she'd wound it up, tinkling music had
played and she'd heard a voice crying for
help. It turned out that the little fairy
figure in the box was a Fairy Queen,
who'd been imprisoned there as a result
of an evil magic spell cast by Sorcero, a
wicked enchanter. She could only move
her mouth and eyes – the rest of her
body was hard and lifeless.

According to Sorcero's spell, only a
true friend to all eight kingdoms could
break the enchantment and free the
Fairy Queen. And so, with her help,
Megan had magically travelled to Silver
City, and had had an amazing adventure
there. Afterwards, when Megan had
returned to her bedroom, she was

delighted to discover that the Fairy Queen could now move her head. By making a friend in Silver City, Megan seemed to have weakened Sorcero's enchantment!

But then, as suddenly as it had started, the magic had stopped and the Fairy Queen had become stiff and unmoving again. Since then, Megan had been waiting excitedly for her to come back to life, but whenever she tried winding the key in the music box, nothing happened. Megan's adventure in Silver City was starting to feel like a strange dream now. She couldn't help worrying that Sorcero had discovered that the Fairy Queen had found help in the human world, and cast another spell to prevent her from coming to life again.

Megan was glad when the school bell rang that afternoon to mark the end of the day. She called goodbye to her friends, and hurried home as fast as she could, racing straight upstairs to her bedroom once she got in.

As she burst into her room, Megan froze. Tinkling music was pouring from

her music box … before she'd even had a chance to wind the key! She shut the door hurriedly and raced over to where the box sat on her dressing table. "Are you there?" she whispered hopefully.

To Megan's joy, the Fairy Queen's eyes sparkled with life, and her mouth turned

up in a smile. "I'm here," she said. "Hello again." She moved her head gingerly from side to side. "Oh, I wish I could stretch. I hate being trapped like this. I so miss being able to fly."

"I thought something terrible must have happened," Megan said. "You've been as still as stone

for the last few days, I was starting to worry Sorcero must have found out, and…"

Megan broke off, aware that she was babbling. The Fairy Queen smiled gently at her. "I'm fine," she said. "But I must see what's happening in my world. I have a horrible feeling Sorcero is up to his tricks once more, and that's what's brought me back to life. Would you be so kind as to touch the end of my wand, Megan, and we'll take a look?"

Megan was only too pleased to help. She touched the tip of the wand, and the Fairy Queen commanded, "Show us Sorcero!"

Goosebumps prickled all over Megan as the wand vibrated between her fingers. Then a flood of silver sparkles whirled

out from it, circling the mirror in the lid of the music box like a glittering wreath. The reflection of Megan's bedroom rippled, before disappearing entirely as a new image took its place.

"It's Sorcero's spell-chamber," said the Fairy Queen in a nervous whisper, as Megan saw a dingy cave appear, draped in cobwebs. The enchanter himself, dressed in a black cloak, was poring over a map on an old wooden table.

He had a long grey beard, a lined, craggy face and a cold glint in his eyes. "So, let's see," he said to himself, peering through his magic magnifying glass at the map. "Has Silver City been brought to its knees yet by that bungling dancing giant? Are they desperate for a clever enchanter to come in and rescue them with his

magnificent magical powers?"

He laughed, but it wasn't a pleasant laugh, thought Megan with a shiver. She knew that Sorcero had once had the Fairy Queen's job of magically righting any wrongs throughout the Land of Eight Kingdoms, and that he had become jealous of her powers and popularity after he retired. By imprisoning her in the music box, he hoped to regain his status and make himself indispensable once more.

Suddenly, Sorcero let out an angry cry and leaned closer over the map. "Wait! This can't be…" he muttered. "Where are the broken buildings? Where is the brainless giant?" He balled one hand into a fist and slammed it down on the yellowing paper, making Megan jump as she watched. "My plan has been foiled!"

"Oh dear," the Fairy Queen murmured. "He's not happy about that."

Sorcero's rage made Megan feel shaky, especially as it was she who'd broken the giant's enchantment and helped save Silver City from being destroyed.

"Those people weren't meant to sort out the problem for themselves," he roared. "I was meant to put everything right for

them. Curses! How did the giant break the enchantment so quickly?" He glared furiously at the map. "I need a better spell," he muttered. "Let me think…"

Megan and the Fairy Queen watched anxiously as Sorcero scratched his chin with a bony finger. Then a glint returned to his eyes and he moved the magnifying glass to a different area of the map. "The Emerald Seas…" he murmured. "I could make a monstrous splash there. The Fairy Queen will get the blame when everything goes wrong, and then I'll appear and save the day. Oh yes – what a hero I will be!"

He gave a horrible cackle, raised his wand and pointed it at the map, muttering a string of enchantments. There was a bright purple flash of light, and then the cave was filled with black smoke.

The Magic Secrets Box

Chapter Two

*M*egan backed away, as if the smoke was going to pour into her bedroom, but then the image in the mirror disappeared. All she could see now was the reflection of her own face gazing in nervously. She bit her lip. "That didn't sound good," she whispered. "What do you think he's planning to do?"

The Fairy Queen looked dismayed. "I don't know," she said, "but I'm guessing you're needed in the kingdom of the Emerald Seas, Megan. If my magic can send you there, will you go?"

Megan felt her heart give a great thump of excitement as she tried to imagine what the land would look like. The Emerald Seas sounded beautiful, the sort of place you saw in holiday brochures. "Wow," she said, then hesitated. Something had occurred to her. "But… Well, I'm not a bad swimmer or anything," she went on. "I've got my hundred-metres badge, but … I don't like being out of my depth for too long, and I can't swim very far underwater…"

The Fairy Queen's eyes sparkled as if something had amused her. "There's no need to worry about that," she told Megan. "You'll be safe in the water, I promise. Are you willing to try and stop Sorcero's mischief?"

"Yes," Megan said breathlessly. "I'll try."

"Thank you," the Fairy Queen said. "Then all you need to do is touch the end of my wand and say 'Take me to the kingdom of the Emerald Seas.'"

Megan took a deep breath, touched the end of the fairy's wand with her forefinger and repeated, "Take me to the kingdom of the Emerald Seas."

A split second later, Megan heard the tinkling music start up again, ringing much louder around her head, and her bedroom began to blur before her eyes. She just had time to hear the Fairy Queen call out, "Good luck!" before she felt herself being pulled through the air, very fast, with bright lights rushing around her in all directions.

After a while, it seemed as if she was slowing and she waited to feel her feet land on the ground once more … but they didn't. Then the world swung fully into focus again and Megan realized why. Her feet had vanished and in their place was a gleaming fish-tail. She'd been magically transformed into a mermaid, with a sparkly green top and pink shell necklace! So that was why the Fairy Queen hadn't been worried about her being out of her depth – she could breathe perfectly well underwater!

"Whoa!" laughed Megan, flicking her tailfin and sending herself skimming through the water at top speed. Being a mermaid was awesome, she thought joyfully, as a shoal of small red fish bustled past. Her hair streamed out behind her as she swam, the water cool and clear against her skin.

The Magic Secrets Box

Then she heard voices and stopped to listen. They were too far away to make out, but Megan remembered how befriending the person who needed her most in Silver City had weakened Sorcero's spell on the Fairy Queen. She was determined to make a friend in the Emerald Seas, too, so she decided to investigate.

She flicked her tail again and whizzed along the seabed, passing waving fronds of seaweed, an enormous scuttling crab and colourful sea urchins. Tiny blue fish darted in and out of rocks as if they were playing tag, and a large flat ray rose majestically through the water ahead. Megan felt tingly with excitement. It was wonderful being in a completely different world.

She slowed down as the voices became louder. She could now see a group of other young mermaids in the distance, perched on a large circle of white rocks on the seabed, deep in conversation. Megan ducked behind a rock, suddenly feeling shy.

The mermaids wore sparkly tops just like hers, but their hair was a range of pastel shades – blue, green, pink and lavender. They all seemed to be listening to one mermaid in particular. She had long lilac hair and a glittery dark purple top and was leaning forward talking excitedly.

"You should have seen the sea monster," the mermaid said. "It looked soooo ferocious. It had massive teeth this big," she went on, waving her arms dramatically to demonstrate, "and fins so huge they could knock a whale off course. It's true!"

Megan felt a shiver run down her spine as she listened to the lilac-haired mermaid's words, and glanced nervously over her shoulder. The sea monster sounded terrifying! *Is this something to do with Sorcero?* she wondered fearfully.

The Magic Secrets Box

Chapter Three

"*D*on't be so silly, Celeste," scoffed a mermaid with pale green hair tied up in a ponytail. "There are no sea monsters in this part of the ocean."

"And even if there were," put in a mermaid with a dark pink bob and a shimmering green tail, "the Fairy Queen would protect us mer-folk from creatures like that. There's nothing to worry about."

"You've got to stop telling tall stories," scolded a third mermaid, with a peach-coloured plait. "You've fooled us before, and we're not falling for any more fibs."

"They're not tall stories, it's all true!" protested lilac-haired Celeste. "I promise!"

A younger-looking mermaid, whose hair was duck-egg blue, looked uncertain. "One of the seagulls told me that the Fairy Queen has vanished," she told the others. "He said that all sorts of strange, magical things have been happening throughout the eight kingdoms. Maybe Celeste *is* right for once. What if there is a sea monster down here, and the Fairy Queen's not around to protect us from it?"

Celeste shot the blue-haired mermaid a grateful look and was just opening her mouth to speak when the first mermaid beat her to it. "You know what gossips the seagulls are," she said dismissively. "They get everything wrong. Come on, we've got better things to do than sit around here listening to Celeste's nonsense all day." And with that, she swam off, the other mermaids following her.

Celeste stayed where she was, her shoulders drooping in disappointment. Megan couldn't help feeling sorry for her and swam out from her hiding place.

"Hi," she said. "I'm Megan. Are you OK?"

Tears were brimming in Celeste's huge aquamarine eyes, but at the sight of Megan she brushed them away with the back of her hand. "Hi," she replied. "I'm Celeste." She peered closer at Megan. "I don't recognize you. Which mer-family are you from?"

"Er…" Megan hesitated, not sure what to say. The Fairy Queen had made her promise to keep secret her reasons for visiting the Land of Eight Kingdoms for fear of word getting back to Sorcero. So she couldn't explain that she wasn't really even a mermaid, and that magic had brought her to the Emerald Seas!

"I mean, are you one of the Rocks, or part of the Neptune clan, or in the Lobsterpot family…?" Celeste waited expectantly, her gaze curious.

"I'm new around here," Megan replied honestly. "I'm part of the Andrews family," she added, feeling as if she ought to elaborate a little. "Um… We're an old family, originally from the north…" Well, it was true, she reasoned. Her grandparents still lived in Scotland, as did lots of her cousins.

Celeste blinked. "I've not heard of them, but welcome to this part of the Emerald Seas," she said. "I suppose you know all about the area … do you?"

"Not really," Megan replied.

"Oh, then you need a guide," Celeste said, perking up. "I can show you round. Come on!"

Megan followed Celeste through what appeared to be a mermaid village, with lots of white rocky houses, their rooftops

decorated with gleaming shells.

"Be on your guard," Celeste warned.
"Watch out for sharks, especially. I got
chased by one the other day but managed
to get away after a terrible struggle. Look –
it got its teeth into my tail."

As Megan stopped to inspect the
shark's toothmarks on Celeste's tail, an
older mermaid swam up to them.

"What's my daughter telling you, then?" she said. "She's got a big imagination, has Celeste."

Megan turned to her. "She was just telling me about the shark bite," she replied politely.

The older mermaid hooted with laughter. "Shark bite? Celeste! We both know that graze came from some rocks, not a shark's teeth."

Celeste turned away, embarrassed and annoyed. "Mu-um!" she said. "Don't listen to her, Megan, come on."

As Megan swam after Celeste, the older mermaid winked at her. Megan was definitely going to take Celeste's stories with a pinch of salt from now on, she decided, but couldn't help warming to Celeste all the same. Plus, she could keep an eye out for any strange goings-on during her tour – Sorcero's spell was sure to be causing trouble somewhere.

First, Celeste showed Megan the mermaid nursery where an older mermaid was instructing some young mermaids on how to practise their diving. Elsewhere, a dolphin was showing another class how to somersault in the water, and an enormous octopus was rocking three baby mermaids to sleep in its tentacles.

Next they came to the mer-palace, a large white building with silver turrets and a grand mother-of-pearl front door. In front of the palace stretched the most beautiful gardens Megan had ever seen, full of brightly coloured sea plants that rippled and shimmered with the movement of the current. "The King and Queen live there,"

Celeste said breathlessly, gazing hopefully up at the windows for any signs of their royal highnesses.

Swimming further out to sea, they passed a group of friendly dolphins who waved their flippers at Celeste. Then they came to a dark, rather spooky-looking jungle of huge seaweed plants.

"What's this place?" Megan asked warily, gazing at the tall green and brown fronds as they swayed mysteriously.

"It's the seaweed forest," Celeste replied. "Best not to go in there; you can get really lost because it's so dark." She lowered her voice. "And I've heard it's full of ghosts."

"Ghosts?" Megan echoed.

Celeste nodded solemnly. "I've never seen one myself, but that's what some of the fish say. Anyway, we're not going that way. We're going straight ahead towards the seahorse stableyard," she said, swimming off. But she hadn't gone very far when she suddenly bounced backwards and let out a cry of shock. "Whoa," she said, trying to swim forward again but failing. "That's weird. Megan, come and see. There's some kind of … barrier here."

Megan followed cautiously, wondering if this was one of Celeste's fibs. But she was right – they could swim no further because a transparent rubbery wall was blocking the way. They swam sideways to check how far the wall went, but it continued on and on as far as they swam.

"I don't understand," said Megan, frowning.

"Nor me," said Celeste. She dived right down, but discovered that the wall went all the way to the seabed. Then she tried swimming towards the surface of the water, and discovered that the barrier arched above them. "This way is completely shut off. I've never seen anything like it before. I—" She stopped and cocked her head. "Did you hear that?" she whispered.

Megan listened. At first, all she could hear was the sound of the seaweed swishing in the water, but then she heard a faint cry coming from deep in the forest. "Help! Help!"

Celeste clutched at Megan's arm, her face suddenly pale. "Oh no!" she said.

"Someone's in trouble."

They raced back to the edge of the seaweed forest.

"Do you think it's one of the ghosts?" Megan asked, her heart thumping. She wasn't sure she totally believed in ghosts, but the forest looked so dark and spooky, anything seemed possible.

"It might be," Celeste said. "Or it might even be someone caught by the sea monster. Whatever it is, we've got to swim to the rescue immediately!"

The Magic Secrets Box

Chapter Four

*J*ust as Celeste was about to plunge through the water into the forest, Megan grabbed her arm. "Wait," she said hurriedly. "Have you really and truly seen a sea monster? Honestly?"

Celeste hesitated. "Well … not actually with my own eyes," she admitted. "One of the sardines told me he'd seen it though, and I do believe him. Come on," she said impatiently. "Someone needs help." She scooped up a handful of pink stones. "We'll leave these as a trail so we can find our way out again."

Megan still wasn't sure about swimming into the seaweed forest and coming face to face with ghosts or a sea monster, but she didn't have much choice. Celeste seemed to have made up her mind that they had to investigate and was already diving through the swaying green fronds, dropping pink stones every now and then to mark her route. Megan hastily swam after her.

The seaweed forest was chilly and gloomy, with little sunlight making it through the thick-growing plants. Megan gazed from left to right as she swam, listening hard for any signs of danger.

"Help! Please! Somebody help!" came the voice again. It sounded young and frightened. Megan hoped they could get to whoever was in trouble in time.

As they swam deeper and deeper into the seaweed forest, Megan noticed that there were no fish or other sea creatures anywhere to be seen. Had they been scared away by the sea monster? She glanced round nervously, expecting to be pounced on at any second.

A few moments later, they came to a clearing where the ground was too rocky for seaweed to grow. And there, stuck in a crevice was a young pink-haired mermaid struggling frantically, her tail flipping from side to side. "Oh, Celeste, thank goodness!" she cried when Megan and Celeste swam towards her. "I thought I was going to be trapped here for ever."

"Sandy!" exclaimed Celeste. "What are you doing here? Let me help you. This is my new friend, Megan, by the way."

"Hello, Sandy," said Megan, swimming over to the young mermaid.

She and Celeste both took Sandy's arms and tried to heave her out of the rocks, but Sandy gave a shriek. "Ow! Not so hard!"

Megan could see that poor Sandy's tail was scraping painfully on the rocks. "Sorry," she said. "We didn't mean to hurt you."

Celeste scratched her head. "I'm not sure how else we can get you out without moving these rocks, and they're way too heavy for us. If only the Fairy Queen was here! She'd be able to use her magic powers to lift the rocks off you."

"How did you end up getting stuck in here anyway?" Megan asked. She knew, of course, that there was no chance of the Fairy Queen coming to the rescue – but she remembered that Sorcero had wanted to play the part of hero. Had he used his magic to trap Sandy? Was he planning to make a grand entrance and rescue her? She shivered at the thought. She was sure that it would only take one searching sweep with his cold, glinting eyes for him to work out what she was doing in the Emerald Seas.

Sandy looked sheepish. "I was exploring," she confessed, "and I got lost."

"You went exploring in the seaweed forest?" Celeste exclaimed. "Are you crazy?"

Sandy hung her head. "One of the

dolphins dared me," she muttered. "I was only going to stay in for a few minutes, but I dropped one of my silver bangles into these rocks and dived down to find it. Then some of them slipped, trapping me here." She sighed. "I'll never get out!"

"Oh yes, you will," Celeste replied. "Because I'm going to get help from the other mermaids. I'm sure we'll be able to push these rocks off you if I can gather lots of helpers. I'd better hurry though, we don't want the sea monster finding you here. He'd gobble you up in seconds."

Sandy looked petrified. "Sea monster? What sea monster?" she asked.

Celeste clapped a hand over her mouth. "Oops. Er … never mind," she said quickly. "Megan, you stay and keep Sandy company. I'll be back as soon as I can."

Celeste swam off, leaving Megan and Sandy in the clearing. "Don't worry, I don't think there really is a sea monster," Megan said kindly once she'd gone. "Celeste hasn't actually seen it herself, I'm sure it's just a silly story."

"I hope so," Sandy said, glancing round anxiously.

Thankfully Celeste was a fast swimmer, and it wasn't long before they saw her speeding towards them again. Unfortunately, she was on her own.

"Where are the others? Are they on their way?" Sandy asked.

Celeste shook her head. "I'm afraid there are no others," she replied, looking downcast. "Nobody believed me when I said you were trapped in the forest, Sandy. They all thought it was a story I'd made up and refused to come with me." She put her head in her hands. "What are we going to do now?"

The Magic Secrets Box

Chapter Five

*M*egan thought for a moment. "Well, if the other mermaids won't help us push these rocks away, we're just going to have to find someone – or something – else who will," she said. "Maybe a strong sea creature – how about a whale?"

"Great idea," Sandy said eagerly, her face brightening. "Whales are really kind. I'm sure one wouldn't mind coming to help."

Celeste looked uncertain. "Hmmm," she said, twisting her fingers together. "I don't know…"

"What's the problem?" Sandy asked in surprise. "It'll only take a few nudges from a blue whale to move the rocks and set me free. They're huge, and really strong!"

"She's right," Megan said. "Come on, Celeste, let's go and find a friendly whale."

Celeste hung her head and mumbled something under her breath.

Sandy and Megan looked at each other. "What did you say?" Megan asked.

"The whales don't like me," Celeste replied, sounding rather sulky. Then, with a guilty shrug, she went on to explain. "I told some of the baby whales a scary story the other day and accidentally gave them nightmares. The mummy whales got really cross and shooed me out of Whale Valley." She sighed. "I'm not exactly their favourite mermaid right now."

"Well, we still have to try," Megan reasoned. "Look, I'll go with you, and you can say sorry. If we're both extra-nice and polite, they might help us out." She turned to Sandy, feeling bad at the thought of leaving the little mermaid on her own. "I promise we'll be as fast as we can."

Sandy's face fell, but then she nodded bravely. "OK."

Celeste and Megan swam through the other side of the seaweed forest, leaving a second trail of stones as they went. It was nice to emerge into the clearer, lighter water once more, Megan thought in relief.

Whale Valley was in a deep part of the Emerald Seas. As they swam nearer, Megan could hear what sounded like singing, although it wasn't like any singing she'd ever heard before. The music was haunting, with high-pitched notes that soared in a melody, then ran all the way down to low grumbles. "What's that?" she asked.

"It's the humpback whales singing," Celeste replied, sounding surprised to be asked. "Gosh, you must be a long way from home if you've never heard that before."

Megan blushed, not wanting to give away her secret. "Mmmm," was all she said. Then in the next moment, her eyes lit up as she caught sight of the first group of whales – vast, grey creatures with barnacled backs and huge sweeping tails. "Wow," she breathed. "Aren't they awesome?"

"Uh-oh," Celeste said, squirming uncomfortably as one of the whales, a cross-looking humpback, spotted her and made a beeline for them. "Here comes trouble."

"You again!" snapped the humpback.

"Didn't I tell you, you're not welcome
here any more? You and your silly stories;
I'm not having you frightening the little
ones again. Go on, shoo!"

Celeste dropped her gaze. "I'm sorry,"
she said. "Really, I am. I won't do it again,
I promise. But, please – we need to talk to
one of the blue whales. Our friend is in
trouble and needs help."

The humpback swished her tail irritably. "This sounds like another of your tall stories to me, Celeste," she retorted. "Why on earth should I believe you?"

"Because it's true!" Megan cried. "Please, we really need help. We wouldn't make up a story about something like this."

The humpback curled her huge top lip as if she wasn't sure whether to believe the mermaids or not. Her eyes rested on Megan, who gazed back as beseechingly as she could, even though the whale's stern face reminded her of Mrs Harvey in a really bad mood.

After what seemed like ages, the humpback finally nodded her enormous head. "Very well," she said. "Most of the blues have gone down to the Deep. Something about an enchanted barrier that's appeared that they're trying to break through. I think Arthur is still around though." She rolled her eyes. "Not that he's much use to anyone, the old grump."

With that, the humpback turned and swam regally away like a mighty cruise ship.

Celeste looked confused. "Another enchanted barrier?" she repeated, frowning. "Very strange. We must send word to the King and Queen once Sandy's free. Come on, let's find Arthur."

Megan followed her into the depths of the valley where they found the most gigantic creature she had ever laid eyes on. The mighty blue whale was as long as at least six buses parked end to end and

Megan felt as small as a shrimp in comparison.

"Er … Arthur?" Celeste called up politely, swimming round to his head end. "Hello there. Have you got a minute?"

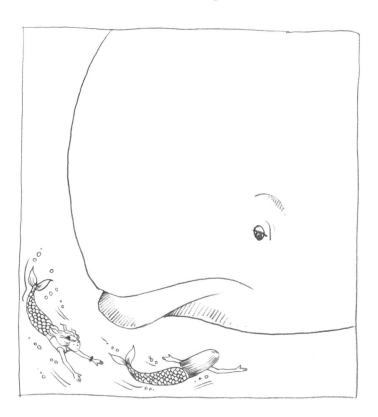

"A minute, an hour, an eternity, what's the difference?" Arthur replied gloomily. "It's all the same to me. Stuck here while the others get to go on an adventure, bashing up an enchanted wall. 'We don't need you, Arthur', they said to me. 'You'll only get in the way.' Typical, that, isn't it? Blooming typical."

Megan and Celeste exchanged a look. Arthur didn't exactly seem in the jolliest of moods.

"Well, actually—" Megan began, but Arthur hadn't finished.

"Just my luck," he complained. "The one day something interesting happens and I have to stay here. Talk about unfair."

"Well, it's funny you should say that," Celeste put in quickly, swimming in front of one of the whale's half-open eyes.

"Because there's something else happening that is much more interesting than an enchanted wall."

Arthur had stopped moaning and seemed to be listening, so Celeste went on. "We were wondering if you could help. You see, one of our mermaid friends is stuck – she was exploring and got lost in the seaweed forest, and—"

"Get on with it," grumbled Arthur.

Megan took over. "We need someone really strong and powerful to push some rocks off a trapped mermaid," she said coaxingly, "and we were hoping you could help us. This is your chance to get involved in a daring rescue adventure!"

"A daring rescue adventure?" Arthur echoed, brightening. "Why didn't you say so before? Of course I'll help!"

Megan wanted to hug him in relief, but it would have been like trying to hug a mountain. She beamed at him instead. "Thank you, Arthur! We'll show you where she is. This way!"

Celeste and Megan led Arthur back along their trail of stones through the seaweed forest towards the rocky clearing. But as they approached, they saw a terrifying sight. Up ahead of them was a giant beast with massive fins and a powerful tail. And it was heading straight for Sandy!

Megan and Celeste watched in horror as Sandy let out a scream. "It's the sea monster," gasped Celeste, and Megan nodded, unable to speak. So there really was a sea monster – Celeste had been right all along!

The Magic Secrets Box

Chapter Six

Megan was frozen with fear and so it seemed was Celeste – but the whale didn't hesitate for a moment. "Pick on a tiddler, would you?" he bellowed, racing after the sea monster. "Oh no, you don't!"

The sea monster turned to face them, and the mermaids shrank back in horror. It was even more terrifying when they could see its huge fanged jaws and mad-looking red eyes. "Say my name and I will disappear!" it commanded menacingly, flapping its fins in a ferocious manner.

"Say my name and I will disappear!"

"I don't care what your name is, just disappear now or you'll have me to deal with," Arthur thundered, plunging towards the sea monster.

"Say my name and I will disappear!" raged the sea monster, lashing out at Arthur. "Say my name and I will—"

"Stop saying that!" Arthur bellowed, pushing the monster away with one swipe of his enormous head. "Swim back off to whichever depths you came from and leave us good sea creatures alone."

The sea monster advanced once more. *Clearly it's not going to give up that easily*, thought Megan with a shudder. Thank goodness they had Arthur there!

"Say my name," the monster wailed, "and I will disappear."

"Why does he keep saying that?"
Megan whispered to Celeste.

"No idea," Celeste replied, "but it's like
he can't seem to stop."

"I know," Megan said, unable to take
her eyes off the sea monster. "It's almost
as if he's been enchanted, or—" Then she
stopped, her own words echoing round
her head. Had the sea monster been
enchanted? Was this something to do
with Sorcero's bad magic?

"Wait!" she called. "Has someone put
a spell on you?"

The monster jerked round at Megan's
words, and Megan was sure his eyes
gleamed hopefully. "Say my name and I
will disappear," he repeated, nodding.

Megan thought back to Olaf the giant
in Silver City who'd been unable to stop

dancing. Just like Olaf, the sea monster seemed trapped by some kind of magic curse, too. "I think he's been enchanted," she said to the others, "and until someone answers his riddle, he can't say anything else." She turned back to the sea monster. "Is that right?"

The monster looked as if he wanted to cry. He'd gone very still apart from his head, which he was nodding frantically. "Say my name and I will disappear," he said again, his eyes darting desperately from Megan to Arthur.

"So we just need to guess his name…" Celeste said. "Er … Squelchy? Mr Tentacles? Fang?"

"Boris," Arthur suggested. "Horace. Doris?"

"Chomper?" Sandy piped up, trembling.

The monster shook his head. "Say my name and I will disappear," he said tearfully.

Megan thought hard. She couldn't help being reminded of the story of Rumpelstiltskin, where the queen had

desperately tried to think of the little man's name. But guessing names could take hours! Unless… Unless the answer to the riddle wasn't actually the monster's name, of course. "Wait," she said, her mind racing. "What if we've got the wrong idea? If it's a riddle, the answer might not be as simple as his actual name."

At her words, the monster's face brightened and he nodded feverishly.

"Maybe it's just a word," Megan went on, trying to reason it out. "You say the word … and whatever the word is, it disappears."

The monster nodded harder than ever and Megan felt sure she was on the right track now, but the others all looked blank.

"Like … vanish? Or invisible?" Celeste suggested.

"Magic," Arthur tried. "Er… Naughty porpoises?"

Celeste raised an eyebrow.

"What?" Arthur said. "You know what those porpoises are like. As soon as you say their name they vanish because they think they're in trouble for something."

The others all began talking at once and Megan couldn't think straight with so much chatter. She put her hands over her ears so as to get some quiet … and then almost immediately, the answer popped into her head. "I think I've got it," she said, with a laugh. "The answer is 'silence'. Because as soon as you say the word 'silence', the silence disappears!" She turned excitedly to the sea monster. "Silence! Am I right?"

The Magic Secrets Box

Chapter Seven

Megan held her breath, crossing her fingers tightly. Then, all of a sudden, the water around the sea monster began to sparkle with purple light. As the sparkles faded, the sea monster raised its tentacles in the air and beamed. "Well done!" he cried. "'Silence' is the right answer to the riddle. Oh, thank you so much. You broke the spell!"

Celeste, Arthur and Sandy all cheered and Megan smiled in relief.

"Brilliant, Megan," Celeste whooped, spinning around in the water.

"Good work," Arthur agreed. "Very clever thinking."

Megan blushed, wishing her teacher could see her now. It wasn't every day a blue whale praised you for being clever, after all.

"I'm sorry I scared you, miss," the sea monster said to Sandy. "I know I might look a bit frightening, but I never would have hurt you. I was just so desperate to have someone solve the riddle and break the spell, but everyone else swam for their lives as soon as they saw me and I didn't get the chance to say it to them. I was so excited to see you trapped there. I thought – she won't be able to escape so she'll have to try and solve my riddle!"

"Talking of Sandy," Megan said, "we'd better set you free, now that we've got

two strong creatures here to push those rocks away."

"Of course! I'd be glad to help," the sea monster said.

He heaved at the rocks while Arthur pushed them with his nose. After just a few moments, there was a rumbling, grating sound and the rocks gave way.

Sandy swam out and turned a somersault in the water, looking relieved. "Thank you so much," she said, smiling shyly at the sea monster and Arthur.

"My pleasure," said the sea monster, bowing his head a little. "The least I could do, now that I'm free from that horrible spell."

"Who put this spell on you in the first place?" Megan asked him. "What happened?" She had a pretty good idea who'd enchanted the monster, but wanted to hear his story.

"Well, I was minding my own business with the other monsters, down in the Mudlands at the bottom of the ocean," the sea monster began, "when I found myself being pulled up to the surface by some kind of magic. There was a man standing on a rock, dressed in a black cloak. He pointed a stick at me and chanted some magic words … and after that, I couldn't say anything except for that wretched riddle. Then he told me he was going to trap me in a giant enchanted dome so that I couldn't get back to my friends. Said something about me terrifying all the other sea creatures, and gave this horrible laugh, as if that was funny."

"An enchanted dome…" Celeste said slowly. "That must have been the strange barrier we found."

Arthur looked concerned. "I wonder who this man is, and why he cast such a spell. He sounds like trouble. Thank heavens you broke the enchantment, Megan." He gave himself a little shake, sending waves crashing out from his enormous body. "Goodness!" he said. "Today is turning out to be quite an adventure! It's definitely the most un-boring day of my life."

Megan smiled, but something had been bothering her. She turned to Celeste and took her hand. "I'm sorry," she said. "I have to admit that I didn't take you seriously when you were talking about the sea monster – nobody did, by the sound of it. We should have believed you in the first place."

Celeste hung her head. "It's partly my fault," she admitted. "If I wasn't always telling my tall tales, everyone would have believed me straightaway, rather than thinking the sea monster had come from my imagination. I guess I've learned a lesson. What with that and scaring the baby whales… Looks like I should keep my stories to myself from now on." She put her arm around Megan. "Thank you, though. You've been a good friend."

Megan smiled at Celeste's words. She was glad to have made a friend in the Emerald Seas, especially one as fun and lively as Celeste. She hoped their friendship would weaken Sorcero's spell on the Fairy Queen, back in the music box.

Arthur gave Celeste a friendly nudge. "You know … I love exciting stories, even if nobody else appreciates them," he said, his eyes twinkling. "You can always come and tell your stories to me – the wilder and more exciting the better!"

Celeste beamed. "Thank you, Arthur. I'd like that very much," she said, and dropped a kiss on his nose.

Arthur blushed.

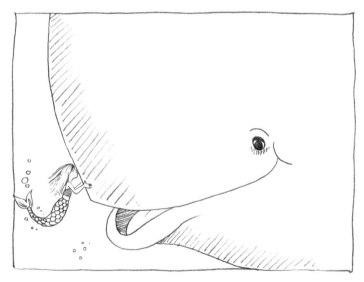

"And it's been lovely to meet you, Mr Sea Monster. What is your name, by the way?" Celeste added.

"Eric," he replied. "Nice to meet you, too. Now, if you don't mind, I'm going to see if that enchanted dome has vanished so that I can return to the Mudlands. Tentacles crossed. Goodbye, everyone."

"I must be off, too," said Arthur, "but don't forget to drop by soon, Celeste, and tell me some of your awesome stories."

He waved his mighty fins and set off for Whale Valley.

Celeste turned to Megan and Sandy. "Let's go back and tell the other mermaids what happened," she suggested. "Although you two had better tell them the full tale. I'm not sure they'd believe me!"

The three mermaids swam back through

the seaweed forest, following the trail of pink stones. *It seems ages since we first swam this way*, Megan thought to herself. So much had happened since her arrival in the Emerald Seas.

Back in the mermaid village, Celeste's mermaid friends were lounging on the circle of white rocks. They seemed rather suspicious when Sandy began recounting her adventure, but by the end of it, they were all open-mouthed with admiration for both Sandy's rescue and the breaking of the sea monster's enchantment.

"Celeste and Megan were so brave and so kind," Sandy said proudly. "And if Celeste ever comes and asks for help again, please believe her, because she's going to be much more truthful from now on!"

"I am," Celeste said quietly. Then she

grinned. "But I don't blame you for not believing me before!"

Everyone smiled and hugged Celeste, and Megan felt really happy for her.

Just then there came a trumpeting sound and the mermaids looked round to see a shiny pink lobster blowing into a conch shell. "All rise, please," he said briskly, "for the King and Queen of the Emerald Seas!"

The Magic Secrets Box

Chapter Eight

*E*veryone immediately swam up from where they'd been gathered on the rocks, then bowed their heads as two very grand figures swept into view. Megan copied Celeste, her heart thumping.

The King and Queen wore crowns of interwoven silver, coral and gleaming pearls, and flowing capes of luminous blue and green that swirled out behind them as they swam. Megan swallowed nervously. They looked very serious.

The Queen swam straight over to

Megan and smiled. "I'm so pleased to meet you," she exclaimed. "I hear you have been brave and clever enough to break the spell controlling an otherwise good-natured sea monster. I am told that the enchanted dome has now vanished, and the sea creatures are free to roam wherever they please once more. Thank you, my dear. We'd like to give you this as a token of our gratitude."

And with that, she placed in Megan's hand a smooth, curving shell that shone pure white against Megan's skin.

"Thank you so much, Your Majesty," Megan said in delight. "It's beautiful."

Just as the words left her mouth, she heard the familiar tinkling melody of her music box. Oh no! When this had happened during her last adventure, she'd been whisked back home moments later.

"It's been lovely to meet you all," Megan said quickly, as the music grew louder, "but I'm afraid I have to return to my family now. Goodbye, everyone. Goodbye!"

She had just enough time to hug Celeste, then swam quickly behind a boulder before the mermaid world began to blur in front of her eyes. She heard faint shouts of "Goodbye!" and "Thank you!" then felt herself whirled away in a dazzling rush of colourful lights. She cried out as she felt the shell fall from her grasp, but she was moving so fast, the sound from her mouth was swallowed up.

Seconds later, her feet touched the ground again. Her feet … she had feet once more! She blinked and looked

around, realizing that she was in her bedroom, and the Fairy Queen was gazing up at her from the music box on her dressing table.

"Hello," Megan said, getting her breath back. She looked at the clock and realized that she'd only been gone a matter of seconds. Then she gave a cry of delight as she glanced back at the music box. "Oh, my shell came with me after all!" For there it was, safely inside the music box, next to the pink ribbon that had been her souvenir from the last adventure.

Megan picked up the shell, which felt warm and dry now. You'd never guess it had been at the bottom of the ocean just moments earlier! She smiled as she put it to her ear and heard the faint roaring of waves. She knew it would always remind her of her friends in the Emerald Seas.

"Well done," the Fairy Queen beamed. "It seems you were successful. And … oh! The tips of my fingers feel normal again."

She wiggled them in delight, a big smile on her face. "Sorcero's enchantment on me is growing weaker, thanks to you. Well done, Megan. You are doing better than I ever could have hoped. Tell me everything."

Megan knelt by her dressing table and told the Fairy Queen all that had happened. When she recounted what the sea monster had said about his enchantment, the Fairy Queen looked worried.

"Hmm," she said. "As with the giant, it seems this spell was used in order to create chaos and fear. It sounds as if Sorcero was hoping to appear at the last minute and save the day so that he'd be a hero to the mer-folk of the Emerald Seas. But instead you were the hero, Megan – good for you."

Megan beamed. "I enjoyed it," she said truthfully. "Well, apart from when I thought the sea monster – Eric – was about to attack Sandy. That was a bit scary. But he turned out to be lovely, he was really—"

"Megan!" came a shout from downstairs. It was Megan's mum. "Come down and start your homework, please."

Megan pulled a face. "I've got some creative writing to do," she said. But then

she brightened. "Actually ... I didn't have a clue what I was going to write about earlier, but meeting Celeste has given me lots of exciting ideas. I might even write a story about a mermaid and a sea monster..."

The Fairy Queen smiled. "That sounds perfect," she said. Then her face tensed and Megan realized that the music from the box was fading away. "I can feel my magic vanishing," the Fairy Queen warned. "Thanks again ... and next time, maybe—"

Suddenly, the light vanished from her eyes and she became stiff and still once more. Megan ran a finger over the Fairy Queen's tiny crown, then carefully placed the smooth white shell back into the box. She smiled and bobbed a little curtsey before the figure of the Fairy Queen.

"Until next time," she said softly, and hurried downstairs. She loved the thought of "next time" – it sounded like the best kind of promise. She wondered where her magic box of secrets would take her ... and what adventures lay in store for her there...

Epilogue

Meanwhile, back in the Land of Eight Kingdoms, in a damp, gloomy cavern, a tall cloaked figure was striding around, his hands behind his back. The sun was sinking low in the sky outside, and several hours had passed since the enchanter had bewitched the luckless sea monster. Sorcero could well imagine what terror and chaos it had brought to the Emerald Seas, trapped as it was in the magic bubble he'd so cleverly conjured. The mer-folk would never trust that the Fairy Queen would come to their rescue ever again, that was for sure.

But have they suffered enough yet? he wondered. Were they ready for a gallant hero to arrive and see off the monster to

make their world safe once more?

"There's only one way to find out," Sorcero muttered to himself. He snatched up his silver-handled magnifying glass and held it over the large map spread out on his table. He positioned it over the Emerald Seas. Sorcero could hear the faint sound of splashing waves and crying seagulls as he moved the magnifying glass over the green wavy lines on the map. But then he frowned.

How could this be? He could see the mer-folk laughing and playing with the dolphins, gathering shells, singing happily and combing their hair. Where was the monster? Where was the enchanted dome?

He slid the magnifying glass further along the map to the area known as the

Mudlands. There was the sea monster clan, floating happily in the murky depths. All seemed peaceful and content. There was no terror or chaos whatsoever.

Sorcero thumped the table furiously, not understanding. His enchantments had been broken again – but *how*? Had his riddle been so easy to solve?

"Next time, I'll cast a stronger spell," he vowed, his eyes caught by the sight of another kingdom on the map. "The Evergreen Woods… I'm sure I could cause some trouble there. Now let me think…"

Some time later, as the sun sank slowly behind the horizon and darkness gathered, the enchanter smiled once more. He had an even better plan this time. And nothing – nothing! – would go wrong…